Tim Barrow Bounty Hunter

Tim Barrow Bounty Hunter
Copyright © 2022 by *Sam Cutrufelli Sr.*

Published in the United States of America
ISBN   Paperback: 978-1-957312-68-2
ISBN   eBook: 978-1-957312-69-9

All rights reserved. No part of this publication may be reproduced, stored in a retrieval system or transmitted in any way by any means, electronic, mechanical, photocopy, recording or otherwise without the prior permission of the author except as provided by USA copyright law.

The opinions expressed by the author are not necessarily those of ReadersMagnet, LLC.

ReadersMagnet, LLC
10620 Treena Street, Suite 230 | San Diego, California, 92131 USA
1.619. 354. 2643 | www.readersmagnet.com

Book design copyright © 2022 by ReadersMagnet, LLC. All rights reserved.

Cover design by Ericka Obando
Interior design by Dorothy Lee

TIM BARROW BOUNTY HUNTER

Ambushed

SAM J. CUTRUFELLI, SR.

ReadersMagnet, LLC

It is springtime and the sun is trying to poke its head out. Then the glory of spring will be fulfilled. The sky will be a platitude of colors such as reds, greens, and blues. The trees have lost their old leaves and new ones are forming—browns, golds, and light and dark greens. Red berries and white blossoms are everywhere. Moisture and dew are rampant. The trail that Tim and his horse Rio are on are wet with moisture. In another half an hour, the sun will dry everything. Suddenly there is a sharp loud crack. Tim knows exactly what it is. Someone is shooting at him. He instinctively rolls off his horse and lies on his stomach on the trail. His mind tells him to not move a muscle. *Please, Tim, do not move. Someone is trying to locate you to tell you. Don't move. They are looking through a telescope mounted on their rifles. Do not move, Tim. If they find you, you're dead; so, do not move. You have some advantages. From the ridge of the trail to where the shooter is, there is a steady decline so they cannot see you. Don't move.* Tim figures the ambusher is young and impatient or he would have waited for him to go forward another twenty feet or so and it would have been a sure shot.

Do not move, Tim. Tim's senses are at their peak. He hears an incredibly low whistle and the shuffle of a horse. Tim figures they are going to use an old Native American Indian truck using a horse to gallop away and the person being shot at will think the shooter has left and expose himself. Tim knows by the horse's gait that the horse is riderless. Another long wait and then Tim hears the creak of someone sitting on his saddle and off they go. Tim strains his ears until there are no more hoof beats on the ground. Tim assumes the shooter is full of nerves and anxious to go to the first bar and have a few shots and beers to calm himself. *Don't move, Tim, because ambushers sometimes work in pairs. There may be another shooter above you.* Tim's instincts were right as presently a horse and rider galloped full speed away. When he thought it was clear, Tim did not move. He still was not sure if there were other ambushers, but he could not lie here forever. Tim had a plan. He would hang onto his stirrups and let Rio drag him out of range but if a shooter saw his arm, he might shoot it and so he waited. Then Tim remembered he had some strips of rawhide in his shirt pocket that were about four feet long. Tim looped one end over his stirrup then tied a knot. Now he still was not exposed so he told Rio to go, and he was dragged out of range. Tim figured he was clear, so he whistled for his mule, Sara, and they left. Tim saw a good, concealed spot where he could leave Sara and the cart. Tim and Rio hurried towards town, to the first drinking hole, hoping his ambusher was there.

Tim could not go into the bar because he was known to the shooter. Tim could not approach the bar as he might be seen so he stopped near a grouping of tall bushes and took out his binoculars to scan the area. There were four horses grouped together and two horses alone further down and tied to a long hitching rail.

One horse was saddled, and one horse was bareback. Tim waits and presently a young man got into the saddle and the two horses left. They were headed towards a rundown miner's shack, so Tim took a back trail and followed. Sure enough, they came to the shack. The ambusher took the two horses inside. Tim waited. He figured the drinks and tension would make the shooter sleepy. Tim was right. He broke down the door and found the shooter sleeping. Tim handcuffed his arms and legs. Then Tim got Rio and brought him into the shack. Tim took some beef jerky out of his saddle bags and leaned up against the building. No one had spoken. After he ate a little, he took some short ropes and tied the shooter to the cot. Better safe than sorry. The shooter was exhausted and did not put up a fight. Tim himself was so exhausted that he fell asleep and was dreaming that Janie called him. *I miss you so I called.*

Janie had been dead for at least two years. Her uncle was the city's schoolteacher and she wanted to visit him. Her uncle sent her money to take the train to Kansas and then to take a stagecoach to Sequoia, Arizona. *When you arrive, I will pick you up.* When Janie arrived, she was told that her uncle left Sequoia for a better job in California. She was now stranded. There was a small café close by, so she went there mostly to sort things out. The owner's name was Carrie and she saw Janie was bewildered and almost in tears, so she went to talk to her. Then the tears did flow as she told Carrie of her plight. Carrie knew her uncle well and she told Janie that she would contact him, but that never happened. Carrie said she had a spare room, and she could stay there until Janie decided what to do. When Janie got her wits together, she told Carrie she would like to stay awhile if Carrie agreed she could help in the café. Tim ate at Carrie's café, so he got to know Janie. She was sixteen and Tim was nineteen. Soon Tim and Janie began dating. It appeared that Tim and Janie were a perfect couple. They loved each other dearly. They talked about marriage. Tim was the local sheriff and part time deputy. At that time, lawmen were not paid much so there was a shortage. So, the government needed a way to slow down crime. They came up with Bounty Hunter and put a decent price on criminals. So, the Sheriff told Tim to try the new system. Wanted posters were placed in post offices and sheriffs' offices. They paid well. A wanted murderer or robber had price tags of five to ten thousand dollars dead or alive. Tim was just getting started. Most of his catches were small time thieves that paid one hundred to five hundred dollars. So, Tim just existed. One morning, Carrie told Tim that Janie did not show up for work. So, Tim went to Carrie's house to find Janie dead. She died in her sleep. She was eighteen years old. Tim was devastated and he left Sequoia. He would live but law breakers, BEWARE! All he wanted to do was to go to work. He missed Janie so much. He was after bigger game. Tim was on his way to Sequoia when he was ambushed.

Tim woke up with a startle. For a minute he lost it, but he looked around and saw his ambusher still there handcuffed and tied. Tim got up but did not talk. He just looked and ate a piece of jerky before he spoke.
He said "What's your name?"
"No name."
"Okay, what is the name of your partner?"
"No partner." No Name asked for a piece of jerky.

Tim said, 'sure' but did not give him any. Tim then started to remove a kerchief that was around No Name's neck. He rolled it up and tied it to No Name's mouth. Tim left to pick up Sara, the mule. When he got outside, he found an old broom. He spread his flour slurry on the ground. When it dried, if someone walked on it, Tim would know if he had a visitor. He rode Rio to where Sara was, got Sara, and they left. mid Sara and Rio is horse.

When he got there, he had a visitor but whoever it was had stopped his horse before he got into the flour. But the horse did get some on his feet enough, so Tim knew someone was waiting for him. Tim waited as he knew he could wait out his shooter. Time passed and no one moved. Then there was a faint bird whistle and a similar reply and then no more. *Just wait.* Finally, a big guy whistled, and a young fellow came out of his nest. The big guy put his finger to his mouth. *Don't talk!* They stood and listened and there was just silence and suddenly the big guy dashed and knocked over the door with his shoulders. Down he went. The big guy and the kid dashed in the shack — no one but tied-down No Name. The big guy told the kid to go outside and stand guard. Before the kid could leave, Tim dashed into the shack, and he rammed his rifle into the kid's stomach. The kid bent over, and Tim hit him on the head with his blackjack. He went down. The big guy had his back to the door. He was trying to untie No Name. Tim ran to the big guy and told him not to move. *Put your arms to your back or I will blow you apart.* The big guy obliged Tim. The big guy was on his knees, so he had no leverage. Tim hand cuffed him. To make sure, Tim rapped him on his head and the big guy was out. Then Tim handcuffed his feet and tied a rope around his waist and secured him to the cot. The kid was coming, too.

Tim handcuffed his hands and legs. *Now what?* Tim was exhausted so he leaned against the wall with his rifle at the ready and he watched and got his breath back. *Excellent job, Tim!* He laughed. Soon the big guys stirred, and Tim took a pillowcase and put it

over his head. He wanted to question the kid. He sat the kid up and asked him his name. At first the kid did not reply so Tim took off the kid's boots and he rapped the sole of his foot with the blackjack.
"What's your name?"
No answer, two more hits on his feet. He started to cry.
"My name is Mason Torrey."
"Okay who is the big guy?"
"I only know his name as Mongo."
"The guy on the cot."
"Don't know him."
"Okay, here is a piece of jerky."

Of course, the kid was hand cuffed, so Tim hand fed him his beef jerky. Tim heard a soft "thank you". He led No Name's horse out and tied his back feet together. Then he took the rope he had around the big guys and fastened it to No Names saddle.

Now he went to find their horses. He then got the riderless horse and tied ropes around his chest and around the cot and he pulled the cost through the door. Tim then maneuvered the cot, so it was about two feet in back of the horse. Then he secured the horses to a stout tree so they could not leave. Tim went to get Rio and Sara and back they went to the shack. Tim secured Sara and left with Rio to find the kid's horse. He was eating the nice green grass with not a care is the world. Tim carefully approached him and offered him some nice ripe apples and soon they became friends. Tim took a short rope and tied him to his saddle and off they went to look for Mongo's horse. Tim found it about two miles from the shack — well concealed and secured. Tim lassoed the horse and again offered up some good apples. Mongo's horse and Tim became friends. He also was tied to Tim's saddle. They went back to the shack. All was as he left it except there was a barefoot boy sitting on a log probably wondering what was going on. The circus must be in town. Tim reached into Rio's saddle bag and got out two chocolate bars. He unwrapped one and took a big bite then he offered the boy the other one.

The boy took the candy bar and started to eat it. Tim asked if he knew where he could buy a wagon. The boy took off. *Oh well.* Tim was in no hurry, but the Fort Sheridan was not close by.

Soon a man came, and he was horse backed and the young boy was on his back end.

The man asked Tim what was going on. Tim said he was a law officer, and he needed a wagon.
The man said, "I have a good one with no horse for twenty dollars."
Tim said "Sold."

The man left and returned with his son and a four-wheeled wagon towed by a mule. Tim looked at it and pulled out twenty dollars then he gave the man ten dollars for the boy and another ten dollars to the man, and they left. Tim got a long stout sapling and tied it to the wagon bed then he tied the kid to the sapling. Next, he prodded Mongo to move to the sapling. He then pulled the cot to the back of the wagon and lifted it onto the wagon bed. With much huffing and puffing he lifted the cot and No Name and pushed him on wagon bed. He tied the cot down so it would not slide out. He then harnessed the riderless horses to the wagon and tied the other horses to the rear of the wagon. Rio and Sara were along the side and off they went. No circus but it had to have a name. Tim was baffled so he let it be. When Tim got near the fort, he tied a white towel to a piece of wood and secured it to the wagon.

When he got to the fort gate he said, "I am Tim Barrow, requesting permission to enter."
The gate opened and Tim was never so happy to see twenty or so awe-stricken soldiers. One soldier went to get the colonel. He said, "That young fellow wants to clean up the whole state all by himself."

The colonel laughed. "Maybe you're right," the Colonel said to the sergeant. "I need you to run a few errands for me. One, find the orderly and have him get some volunteers to air out a small unit for Mr. Barrow. Two, see the cook and tell him Mr. Barrow will be my guest for dinner. Three, see the quarter master and have him supply Mr. Barrow with two sets of
fatigues. Four, find the provost Marshall and tell him to see me. Five, have the stable take care of his animals."

The sergeant left to fulfill all the orders. The colonel and Tim talked, and Tim related his encounters with the ambushers. Tim apologized for not having gotten them to give him their real names. The colonel said that the provost marshal would find out everything. The colonel told Tim he would be his guest for dinner then he left. When he got to his office, colonel saw that the provost marshal were waiting for him outside his office.

"Come in," said the Captain. "We have a couple of challenging cases that Mr. Barrow brought in. Talk to Tim and see what you can do."

The captain saluted and they left to go see Tim. Tim told Captain Parker his story. He said they recognized the two men but not the young kid. They would check his fugitive wanted posters and get back to the colonel. No Name and Mongo were bad apples. No Name was wanted for two murders in Mississippi. He was apprehended and sentenced to hang but he escaped with nineteen other fugitives from a jail in Texas.

Two guards were killed, and it had been three years before Tim had got him. Mongo was wanted for murders of his fiancée and his mother. He was a former pro wrestler — no championships but he was good. There was no record of the kid. The colonel was pleased by the quick findings of his provost marshal. The colonel requested that the two be put in maximum security cells under twenty-four-hour watch. As for the kid, Tim said "He was very polite and if given the opportunity, he could probably be saved."

The colonel recommended the kid be enrolled in the fort's orphanage system and he would be carefully watched. That evening, Tim arrived at the colonel's quarters for dinner. It was a big three-storey home that was moved to the fort for the its senior officer and his family. They had dinner. They retired to the living room to have drinks and cigars and talk.

Tim was given two reward vouchers for his captures — one was ten thousand dollars for No Name and five thousand dollars for Mongo. The fort had a fund for fugitives that were brought in that did not have a wanted poster. The colonel gave Tim three thousand dollars from the fund for the kid. The fort would be reimbursed. This fund was to pay bounty hunters for their captures. The colonel expressed his gratitude to people like Tim for devoting their time and efforts to clean up the state. He also told Tim that there were only two major gangs around Sequoia — one was a gang of three and the other was a gang of four and the boss was a woman that wore a black veil.

"The Captain will give you the particulars."

Tim said, "Good night."

"Good night because old people need their rest! I will see you tomorrow."

Tim left feeling immensely proud that he got to meet Colonel Beckamel. He left by foot. His plan was to go back to his home, town of Sequoia and rest. In the back of his mind, he wondered how and if he would pursue investigating and capturing that mysterious black veiled woman and her gang.

THE END.

BLACK VEILED LADY

My name is Elizabeth Wilkinson. I am approximately fifteen years old. I lived with my mother and father on a ranch on the outskirts of the town of Sequoia, Arizona. Today I have no family, no home. This is my story. Today was one of the worst storms I have ever experienced. It was freezing rain with heavy winds and storming with lightning and thunder. My father and I were having breakfast and the door of the barn kept slamming open and banging shut. My father said the storm would blow the barn door off its hinges. I told my father I would put on my boots and poncho to go bolt the door. This saved my life because the worst tragedy of my young life took place.

My uncle Frank Wilkinson killed my father his brother and my mother and burned down the house and stable. But I am getting ahead of this story. The storm created the equivalence of a war zone. We were all scared that the storm would blow the roof off. My father was very frail, and my mother was on her last days so we were all scared and helpless. Inside the barn was my father's horse and buggy that he drove to work before he became so sick. The animals were really frightened so I calmed them down by talking to them and feeding them their favorite snack of half of an apple each. They did really calm down. Suddenly I heard horses outside. They were close. So, I hid behind some boxes and waited. Two riders drove into the barn. I recognized my uncle's voice. He sounded very drunk and quarrelsome. He kept swearing and yelled at his companion to go and sit on the porch and he would go inside.

"I will go inside and get some food and alcohol!" He banged on the door. My father did not answer so Uncle Frank kicked it open. Jeb sat on the porch bench, very drunk, Frank was big and strong when he was drunk; he was mean. So, Jeb knew to stay clear of Frank. I could tell where Jeb was because of the light on his cigarette. I always knew where Jeb was. My uncle was constantly screaming at my father and mother. I heard him hit my father and knock him down. My mother was so disoriented that she did not know what was happening and Frank was so drunk he did not know how far gone she was. My father kept his army guns in a sack in the barn. So, I got out his scatter gun which was already loaded. I intended to shoot Frank and Jeb. Suddenly Jeb came off the porch screaming and running towards the barn. He must have seen me, so I shot him, but the shot was so low that it hit Jeb in the leg. He went down hard, face first into a pool of cold muddy water. His gun flew out of his hand and landed in another pool of cold muddy water. Before Jeb could move, I put a rope over my father's horse and grabbed the reins of my uncle's horse and Jeb's and the three of us flew out of the barn. There were lots of shots coming at me and I did not even know from where. I just kept moving fast. I knew that my uncle and Jeb could not follow me as their horses were gone. The only guns they had were their body guns. The rifles were still on their horses headed for the cave at the side of the mountain.

I went there often before to shoot birds and small animals such as rabbits and squirrels. Neither Frank nor Jeb knew of my refuge so I was safe. The area was a refuge for birds, small and large and animals such as bears and deer. There were two mountain ranges back-to-back. My mountain was where the cave was, but I am sure there were other caves. Mine had a live waterfall plus many live springs, so the lake was never dry. The lake was large, and it narrowed to form a rambling river. When I used to come here, it was to hunt some food for dinner like duck, geese, or rabbits. When I brought dinner, I was a hero.

On the other side of the lake was a small Indian tribe. There were two that came to my side when they saw me. They were brother and sister. The sister was about my age, and the brother was about ten or eleven years old. He was born deaf and could not talk. His name was Jail Blue. They hunted with bows and arrows. When I visited, I taught Laura how to shoot a gun. She learned fast, and she became very skillful. Now my main objective is to become very skillful with firearms. I shot at flocks of ducks and birds of all descriptions. I did not have a pointer dog so whatever I shot at I had to hunt for.

I was living with nature, but I had Jeb and Frank's bedrolls, so I was plenty warm and cozy. Laura had taught me how to make smokeless fires so I could cook my meals. Jail Blue loved to fish, and I always had trout or bass on the menu. Laura also taught me how to de-feather a bird. She also brought me a large pot plus a skillet, so we had rabbit stew. It was so good. I did not know the full extent of the tragedy until Laura told me.

My father rented most of his acreage to a young Indian farmer. His name was Andy. He told Laura that both my parents were shot to death in the ranch house and the stable was burnt to the ground. Andy told the sheriff he was not there, but a witness said they saw two men and a mule, but he was not able to identify them. No one knew where I was when the sheriff inquired. They noted the tragedy was still stewing and I was thankful that I knew of the cave.

When I arrived, I was so exhausted, but I had to hide the horses as a precaution. The cave was well concealed with tall grass and plants. I took the three horses to the mouth of the cave. I removed the saddles and watered them. I was doing all this instinctively because I was so exhausted, When I woke up, it was the next day. The saddle the saddle bags and other stuff that were carried by the horses were still in a pile where I put them. I had no desire to examine what might be in the saddlebags or the pile of stuff that Frank and Jeb carried. Each saddle had two beautiful rifles. These I hid and repeatedly I vowed that Frank and Jeb would pay.

One day I knew I would have to have the courage to sort Frank's and Jeb's belongings. I thought there might be some letters with addresses or any leads that I could follow up on. I found the saddlebags full of money, gold, and jewelry. I was rich, but not thankful of my bounty. I would gladly trade everything to have my father and mother. I knew I had to learn more about these two. I knew that they were well-trained men, strong and healthy. I had to learn more and practice my skills. I do know that I cannot let this episode in my life consume me. So now where does it go from here?

The story continues with the entrance of Gerald Barrow, Chet Roman, and Colonel Bechamel. All three had listed into the army at the same time. Gerald finished his preliminary schooling, and he was now Sergeant Barrow. Artillery Chet Roman was a private and assigned to Provost Marshal and Colonel Bechamel. He had two years of college. All three were sent to Fort Sheridan. Barrow was run over, and his legs were damaged, so he was discharged with a small disability pension. He was in the army for three years. Roman completed his full term of three years but did not resign. The Colonel went on to be a career soldier.

Roman became a sheriff and fifteen years later they were all still friends. Barrow's wife died early, and they had one son, Tim Barrow. Roman's wife was sick constantly and Colonel Bechamel did not ever marry.

Through the course of time, Roman often deputized Barrow to assist him when he needed experience. He had two other salary deputies, but they had no amount of field experience. They were city police officers. Tim Barrow was taught how to shoot all kinds of firearms. He was taught how to ride and how to rope at age fifteen. And he was good – very good. Sheriff Roman deputized Gerald Barrow and they set out to capture two outlaws as they heard that they were harbored in a deserted railroad shack. They were Frank Wilkinson and Jeb Kramer. They were both wanted dead or alive for the murder of Frank's brother and his brother's wife. There was a shootout and Gerald Barrow was killed. Sheriff Roman was critically wounded, and he eventually lost his left arm. The two outlaws escaped.

Rumors were flying that Frank and Jeb were part of the black veiled lady — a gang of four. If indeed that was true, then the black veiled lady was contradicting her orders of no killing. Frank and Jeb were wanted fugitives for murder. Now, the rumor was Frank and Jeb had killed Gerald Barrow. The black veiled lady's only defense was that the gang never ever kills while engaged in one of her criminal activities. She would abort the robbery than have to kill to succeed. To prove her point, the gang was at one time six.

Two defied her orders and did kill during a botched robbery of a stagecoach and now she only had a gang of four. The two that defied her were set packing and gone. Tim Barrow he would not rest until Frank and Jeb were either dead or incarcerated. Tim's first step was to talk to Lieutenant Colonel Bechamel and get whatever was in the files of Frank and Jeb. Fort Sheridan was the prime Arizona headquarters to stamp out crime.

Tim had some leads. Frank and Jeb had been active, but Jeb was still not fully healed after he was shot during a robbery, so Frank had been active by himself. Jeb could control Frank's drinking and bullying but when Jeb is not there, he gets into fights. So, it is easier for Tim to keep track of Frank. Right now, he was near the Nevada state line, living with a prostitute. Tim was twelve steps behind but if Frank was not active, he would be able to catch up. Tim found where the prostitute lived so if Frank was still holed up with her, Tim had a good chance of apprehending Frank. Tim waited for Frank to make a move but there was none. He saw the woman a few times but no Frank. After three days of surveillance, he figured Frank was not around. So, he knocked on the door of the woman's home. She was drinking and not very coherent. Tim gave her a one-hundred-dollar gold coin. She whooped and danced saying it was her lucky day. Tim asked for Frank. A mouthful of curses came out as she told Tim he beat her badly, so she told him to leave. She was half dead. So, when

Frank was just getting ready to mount his horse, she shot him good in both legs with her scatter gun. She did not kill him, but he was badly hurt and left. It was assumed that he had left in a hurry and ran to the one doctor in town. Tim located the doctor's office and there was one horse reined to a small hitching rail. The horse was large and black—the type that Frank liked. So, Tim reined his horse, Rio, around the corner as he did not want to expose himself. He opened the doctor's door and went in.

The doctor was lying on the floor shot in the chest. Frank was unconscious on a gurney. Tim handcuffed Frank then he went to the doctor. The doctor said Frank shot him because he told Frank that he would have to amputate his legs, or he would die in hours. Tim carried Frank to his horse and managed to lay him across the saddle. Frank was unconscious. He led Frank and his horse around to where Rio was and his mule, Sarah. Sarah was towing a two-wheeled cart. So, they all left. Tim stopped about a mile away to check on Frank. Frank was dead. Tim headed for Fort Sheridan.

It would be a long trip. On the way he would occasionally see a rider shadowing him—always about two miles away, always hidden but Tim knew he was there. He finally approached the road that led to the fort. Suddenly there was a shot and Tim fell off his horse. The shot killed one of two armed men, Tim shot the other man. Above him was movement so he shot at it, and he heard a scream. He circled the mountain and thought that he had hit a girl. He found her and handcuffed her not knowing which side she was on. Tim said he needed to see how badly she was shot and where. She was dressed in faded jeans and one leg of the jeans had a long crease cut with blood. She was on her stomach. He asked her if he could unbuckle her belt to examine the wound. She said no. So, Tim gagged her and rolled her on her back and unbuckled the belt and lowered her trousers. There was a long crease where the shot grazed her, and it was not deep, but it needed disinfecting. Tim tied her feet then tied the rope to a small bush. He told her not to move, that he would be right back. When he started down the hillside, he saw his shadow about two or three miles away. He hid when Tim saw him. Tim found a small first aid bag. Alongside was a pint of 100% whiskey.

He took both as he also checked the ambushers. They were both dead. He would see to them later after the girl. On the way back, he saw movement and he waited. A man with a rifle was trying to find a better shooting spot. Tim waited and the man exposed himself. Tim shot and the shooter was dead instantly. Tim went to the body. He very seldom missed. He went back to the girl. He told her it that it would burn but that it had to be done. She nodded. He poured the whiskey on the wound, and she tried to scream despite the gag. He applied some iodine. It burned but not as much. He let her calm down, put some gauze and tape, pulled up her trousers, and removed the gag. She said thank you and Tim nodded.

"another person is trying to get us. Do not look around but there is a rider up there and he does not know I see him. He has been tailing me for fifteen or twenty miles. I found a spot with some cover, and I dug a small hole and built a fire."

The girl was grateful. Tim said it was getting dark, so he better check on his animals. The girl asked if she was going to be handcuffed forever. Tim said no, removed the cuffs, and left. He rubbed down Rio, fed him, watered him, and did the same for Sarah. He found the ambusher's horse and brought them to where Tim hid the body. After Tim had fed Sarah and Rio, he grabbed some food and went to the girl. They both had bacon and eggs and plenty of hot coffee. It was nice. He asked her name and she said it was Elizabeth. He told Elizabeth that he figured the shadow guy would pay them a visit tonight because he knows they would be going to the fort. So, he was going to set a trap.

Tim gathered some straw and formed two fake bodies and threw some blankets over them. Then he got Elizabeth safely out of harm's way and covered her up cozy and left to wait. Sure enough, about midnight, this big black horse and rider came out of the trees and started shooting at the straw bodies. Then Tim appeared. He shot at Jeb and shot the gun out of his hand.

SAM CUTRUFELLI SR.

Tim said, "If you move, you are dead. Slowly get off your horse and get on your stomach with your hands behind you. Now!"

Jeb was slow so Tim shot at him again this time hitting him in the thigh. When Jeb did not do what he was told Tim then threw a small net over him, then he hit him on the head with his blackjack—not hard, just enough so that Jeb would be out long enough for Tim to secure him. After he had cuffed his feet together, he cuffed his hands then he dragged Jeb between two stands of trees. His legs and hands were then tied to the tree, and then he went to check on Elizabeth. She was no crybaby but when she heard Jeb's voice, it all came back to her in a moment. She had no father, no mother, and no home. Tim brought her a hot cup of tea and she felt better. Jeb was a follower. Tim asked Jeb why he was shadowing him and for so many miles. Jeb said that their boss had something on her mind because she wanted a special meeting. Usually all of us met every two months and we would split the loot four ways. She never took a share—not one cent. Jesse and Rico had to be notified so he was asked to make the trip and Frank stayed behind. It was his job to melt the gold chandeliers and gold cups into gold bars. It was a big task, but Frank always did it.

"So, I took off two weeks and met when we got there. The house was burned down and the shaft that the old squaw lived in was not burned down but there was no sign of her. Frank got all the loot and

left, and we did not know where—Mexico, Canada? I knew Frank better than Jesse or Rico, so the boss lady gave me twenty-five hundred dollars to find him. I wanted him alive, and I knew if Frank was leaving the country, he would party first, so it should be easy, but it was not. I kept track of you because your first concern was Frank. You got your break from the prostitute, and I was right behind you. So, you got Frank at the doctor's office. I visited the woman to find out where you went but I found her dead from Frank's beatings. She had a one-hundred-dollar gold piece. There was no other money. Frank might have stolen it. So, I hired the three gringos to grab you but not kill you as I thought you might know where Frank hid the loot. So here I am. You are the winner."
Frank was a monster.

The next day, Tim made Elizabeth some oatmeal and she enjoyed it very much. Tim started to gather the horses when a soldier from the fort rode up. He knew Tim and he said he would notify the colonel. Tim asked for a wagon and the soldier took off. It was not an exceptionally long wait. A contingent of one large wagon and five heavily armed soldiers arrived. Tim had all the bodies laid out, so it was a matter of minutes to load the wagon. Three armed soldiers climbed the hillside and half-carried and half-dragged Jeb to the wagon where he was securely roped to the wagon.

Tim told the Sergeant that he would escort the horses of which there were many. Elizabeth had two horses. The lone ambusher had one. Jeb's black horse and Frank's black horse and the two other ambushes had two so there was a total of seven. The guns and saddle bags were put in Sarah's cart. Miscellaneous boots, hats and clothing were put in the wagon.

When Elizabeth met the colonel, she was enchanted. She told Tim that the colonel is a dream from heaven and that the he was a master of efficiency. Tim and Elizabeth were set-up in housing and were given clean clothes and their horses were watered and fed.

"We had a wonderful meal at the colonel's residence," Elizabeth said. The Colonel told him she was fine. The following morning, they left in a two-seated wagon pulled by two horses. Eight horses, roped in pairs, were tied to the back of the wagon. Saddles and all other gear were in the wagon. Off they were, bound for home, with Sarah and their cart plodding along in the rear.

THE END.

Printed in the USA
CPSIA information can be obtained
at www.ICGtesting.com
LVHW020232100424
776964LV00026B/509